Little Stories
for
Bedtime

A catalogue record for this book is available from the British Library

Published by Ladybird Books Ltd
27 Wrights Lane London W8 5TZ
A Penguin Company
© LADYBIRD BOOKS LTD MCMXCIX
Stories in this book were previously published by Ladybird Books Ltd
in the *Little Stories* series.
LADYBIRD and the device of a Ladybird are trademarks of Ladybird Books Ltd

*All rights reserved. No part of this publication may be reproduced,
stored in a retrieval system, or transmitted in any form or by any means,
electronic, mechanical, photocopying, recording or otherwise,
without the prior consent of the copyright owner.*

Little Stories
for
Bedtime

Ladybird

Introduction

Children will have sweet dreams after listening to these charming little stories.

Each of the little characters in this book is faced with a big problem. But each of them soon shows that being little doesn't mean you can't be brave or bold, clever or kind…

Contents

Cheeky Little Kitten

by Joan Stimson
illustrated by Jan Smith

Brilliant Little Elephant

by Joan Stimson
illustrated by David Pace

Little Red Car

by Nicola Baxter
illustrated by Colin Reeder
and David Melling

Noisy Little Truck

by Nicola Baxter
illustrated by Harmen van Straaten

Forgetful Little Fireman

by Alan MacDonald
illustrated by Philip Hopman

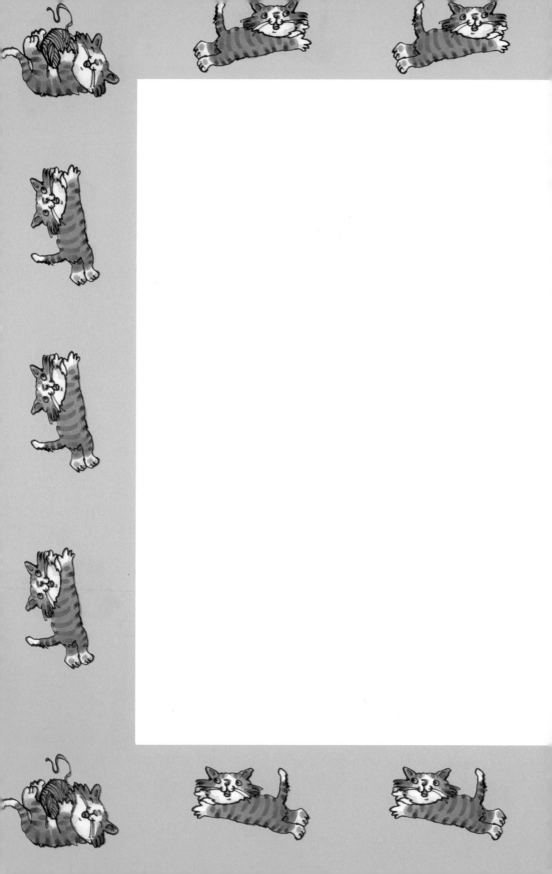

Cheeky
Little
Kitten

Little Kitten was the cheekiest, cheeriest cat in the entire neighbourhood. He thought up the most brilliant games. He never ran out of jokes and, whenever Little Kitten was around, it was almost impossible… not to smile.

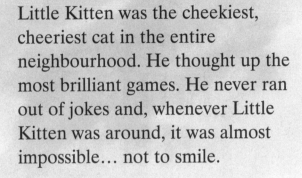

Tee hee hee!

But one day a new tabby cat came to the neighbourhood. She was snooty and sniffy. She was vain and a pain. And right from the start the new cat made it clear. She was too busy worrying about her looks to enjoy herself.

"Don't take any notice," said all Little Kitten's friends.

Have you heard the one about...

But Little Kitten couldn't bear to think of anyone not having fun. So next day he bounded up to the new cat with a cheerful,

> *"Tabby Scowler, come and play.*
> *Try a smile and make my day!"*

And then he began to tell his cheekiest puppy joke.

Little Kitten's friends laughed so loudly that he could hardly hear himself speak. Tabby Scowler thought the joke was funny too. But then she remembered.

"I've just arranged my whiskers. And, if I have a good laugh, they'll get in a tangle again."

So, instead of joining in, Tabby
Scowler simply scowled some more.
And stuck her nose in the air.

I mustn't get my whiskers in a twist.

Little Kitten was disappointed. But next day he bounded up to the new cat with a cheerful,

*"Tabby Scowler, come and play.
Try a smile and make my day!"*

And then he began to describe his latest game.

"It's called *Run, Wriggle and Roll*," said Little Kitten.

His friends were already purring expectantly. But Tabby Scowler looked confused. So Little Kitten explained.

"Run round the garden, wriggle through the hedge and roll down the bank."

Whoooosh! The other cats all rushed off together.

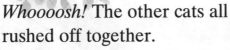

Don't get left behind, Tabby Scowler!

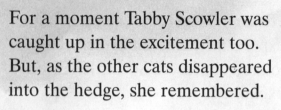

For a moment Tabby Scowler was caught up in the excitement too. But, as the other cats disappeared into the hedge, she remembered.

"I've just washed my fur. And, if I wriggle and roll, it will get all messy again."

So, instead of joining in, Tabby
Scowler simply scowled some more.
And stuck her nose in the air.

Why doesn't
she join in?

Little Kitten was shocked. But that evening he bounded up to the new cat with a cheerful,

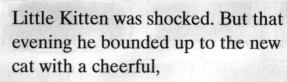

"Tabby Scowler, come and play.
Try a smile and make my day!"

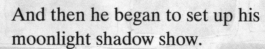

And then he began to set up his moonlight shadow show.

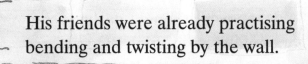
His friends were already practising
bending and twisting by the wall.

Look at me!

I'll make
a monster
shadow.

Tabby Scowler thought perhaps she could make an exciting shadow shape too. But then she remembered.

"I've just draped myself elegantly over the wall. And, if I twist my tail into a snake, I might not be able to make it elegant again."

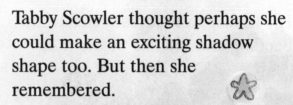

So, instead of joining in, Tabby
Scowler simply scowled some more.
And stuck her nose in the air.

How
undignified.

Little Kitten was beside himself.

"Don't give her a second thought," said all his friends.

But Little Kitten was determined.

"I'll make that cat enjoy herself," he announced, "if it's the last thing I do."

Next day Little Kitten waited patiently for his chance. And that afternoon he *crept* up to the new cat… in total silence.

The sun was warm. And Tabby Scowler was taking a cat nap.

"If I can just find her tickle spot," thought Cheeky Little Kitten to himself, "then she's bound to burst out…"

Now, where's that tickle spot?

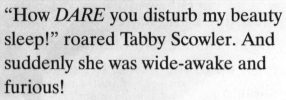

"How *DARE* you disturb my beauty sleep!" roared Tabby Scowler. And suddenly she was wide-awake and furious!

Tabby Scowler chased Little Kitten right round the garden. She leapt after him as he dived for the safety of the hedge. And, when he rolled head over paws down the bank, Tabby Scowler somersaulted after him.

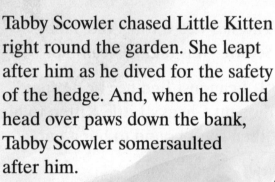

By the time she caught up with Little Kitten, Tabby Scowler was a changed cat.

"He's gone too far this time," groaned all Little Kitten's friends.

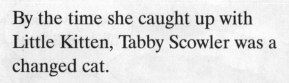

I'm sorry...

"Shall I help you re-arrange your whiskers?" asked Little Kitten.

"*NO!*" bellowed Tabby Scowler. "I'm enjoying myself far too much to worry about my whiskers," she explained. "And after that *AMAZING* chase, I'm in the mood for a good joke."

I haven't had so much fun for ages!

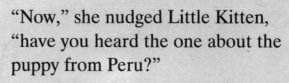

"Now," she nudged Little Kitten, "have you heard the one about the puppy from Peru?"

Little Kitten shook his head in astonishment.

"Well," went on the new cat,

> *"There once was a puppy I knew,*
> *Who lived on the plains of Peru.*
> *He wasn't too bright,*
> *But he danced every night*
> *As he dined upon dinosaur stew!"*

Then she rolled around the grass in hysterics.

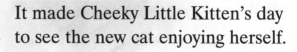

It made Cheeky Little Kitten's day to see the new cat enjoying herself.

And, from then on, whenever he thought up a new game, Little Kitten could be sure… that Tabby *Smiler* would be the first to join in!

Brilliant
Little
Elephant

As soon as she heard the brilliant news, Little Elephant couldn't stop talking about it.

The Head of the Herd had announced the date for the Big Show. And this year Little Elephant was allowed to join in.

Little Elephant skipped round Mum and squealed with excitement.

I'm just a beginner,
But I'll be a winner,
And I'll be the star
Of the show!

"You'd better decide what you're going to do," smiled Mum. "And start practising."

Little Elephant set off straightaway
in search of ideas.

"Look at me!" cried Little Elephant's
cousin from the side of the lake.
"I've made some mud balls. And
I'm juggling."

Little Elephant watched eagerly.
"That's brilliant!" she squealed.
"Let *me* try." Then she made some
mud balls herself.

I'm just a beginner,
But I'll be a winner,
And I'll be the star
Of the show!

But juggling was harder than it looked. One by one the mud balls biffed Little Elephant on the nose.

"OUCH!" she cried. Then she dived into the lake to get clean.

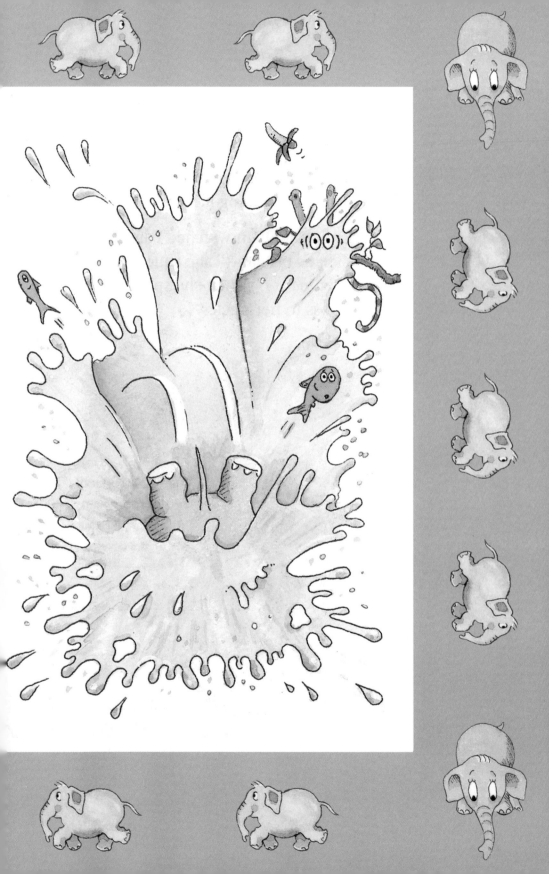

"Look at us!" cried Little Elephant's uncles from the middle of the lake. "We're swimming in time together."

Little Elephant watched eagerly. "That's brilliant!" she squealed. "Let *me* try." Then she splashed across to her uncles.

I'm just a beginner,
But I'll be a winner,
And I'll be the star
Of the show!

But swimming in time was harder than it looked. And soon all the uncles were out of time, too.

"Sorry!" cried Little Elephant. And she swam to the side of the lake to give her uncles some space.

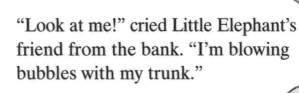

"Look at me!" cried Little Elephant's friend from the bank. "I'm blowing bubbles with my trunk."

Little Elephant watched eagerly. "That's brilliant!" she squealed. Then she dipped *her* trunk in the water. "Let *me* try," she burbled.

But blowing bubbles was harder
than it looked. The water went right
up Little Elephant's trunk. And she
ran sneezing along the shore.

"Look at us!" cried Little Elephant's aunties from a branch overhanging the lake. "We're doing gymnastics."

Little Elephant watched eagerly. "That's brilliant!" she squealed. "Let *me* try." Then she scrambled up beside her aunties…

But, when Little Elephant looked down, she froze with fright. She didn't want to do gymnastics after all.

"Never mind, Little Elephant," said her aunties. "There must be *something* you can do in the show."

I'm just a beginner, But...

But Little Elephant was no longer sure. And, suddenly, she wanted her mum.

"Look at me!" cried Mum, as
Little Elephant trudged into view.
"I'm perfecting my song and dance
routine."

Little Elephant listened intently as
Mum sang a complicated tune. She
looked longingly as Mum's toes
twinkled across the grass.

"Why don't you join in, Little Elephant?" said Mum.

But Little Elephant shuffled and shook her head.

"It's too difficult," she wailed. "I've tried out *all* the acts," she explained. "But I can't do *any* of them!"

Little Elephant's mum stopped dancing and began to think.

At last she had a brilliant idea.

"I know what you can do, Little Elephant," she beamed.

And off they went to the Head of
the Herd to arrange it.

On the night of the Big Show the elephants all gathered by the lake.

"I wonder what Little Elephant's going to do?" they whispered to each other.

Then, as the moon rose, Little Elephant herself appeared in the centre of the display area. And, when at last the audience was silent, she squealed with pride.

Well, don't you look great?
And you won't have to wait
For more than a quick 'hello'.
Though I'm a beginner
Each act is a winner...

And we've got a BRILLIANT show!

"HOORAY!" cried all the elephants. "Little Elephant is going to be the PRESENTER!"

And, because talking was what Little Elephant did best, she introduced every single act… BRILLIANTLY!

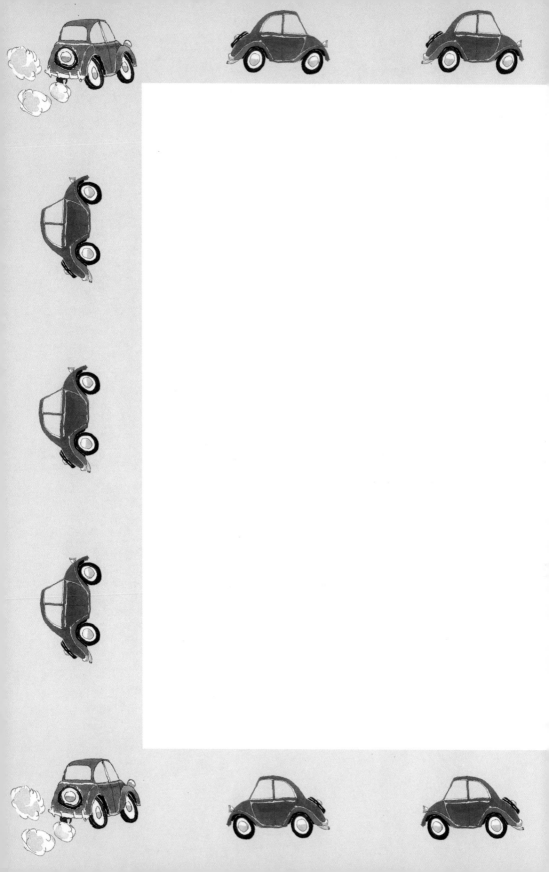

Little
Red Car

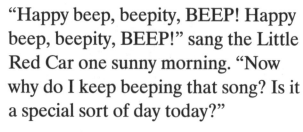

"Happy beep, beepity, BEEP! Happy beep, beepity, BEEP!" sang the Little Red Car one sunny morning. "Now why do I keep beeping that song? Is it a special sort of day today?"

Just then Mike-the-Mechanic's pick-up truck went clanking past. "Hurry up, Little Red Car!" called Mike-the-Mechanic. "Gary-at-the-Garage is expecting you *any minute now*!"

"Well wiggle my wipers!" thought the Little Red Car. "I can't be late for my service! I *knew* something important was happening today."

She didn't waste one more minute. With a beep, beepity, BEEP! she whizzed off down the road.

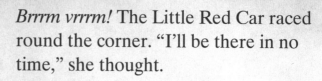

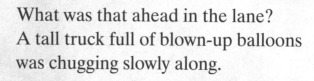

Brrrm vrrrm! The Little Red Car raced round the corner. "I'll be there in no time," she thought.

But suddenly…

What was that ahead in the lane? A tall truck full of blown-up balloons was chugging slowly along.

"Beep, beepity, BEEP! Excuse me!" cried the Little Red Car. "I'm late for a Very Important Appointment. Can't you go any faster?"

But the truck was going as fast as it could. It just chugged steadily on.

The Little Red Car brrrmed and
beeped behind the truck until... *at
last*... it pulled into a lay-by. "*Brrrm
vrrrm!* Watch my wheels whizz now!"
said the Little Red Car.

But suddenly...

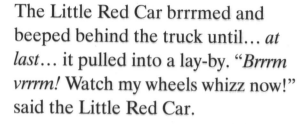

What was that on the road ahead?
A baker's van was crawling carefully
along.

"Beep, beepity, BEEP! Hurry up!"
called the Little Red Car. "Is that as
fast as you can go? I've got a Most
Important Meeting!"

But the van came to a bumpety bump
bit of road and went *even* slower.

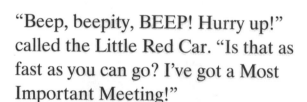

The Little Red Car brrrmed and beeped behind the van until… *at last*… the road widened and she could pass. "*Brrrm vrrrm!* You won't see me for dust!" said the Little Red Car.

But suddenly…

What was that ahead? A blue truck loaded *full* of tooters and hooters and bangers and clangers was trundling along.

"Beep, beepity, BEEP! Get a move on!" cried the Little Red Car. "A snail could go faster than this!"

But the blue truck, with its heavy load, was going as fast as it could. It just kept trundling along.

The Little Red Car brrrmed and beeped behind the blue truck until… *at last*… it pulled into a gateway and she could zoom past. *"Brrrm vrrrm! Full steam ahead!"* said the Little Red Car.

But suddenly…

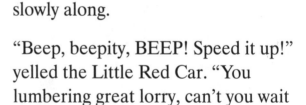

What was that right across the road? An Extra Wide Load was moving slowly along.

"Beep, beepity, BEEP! Speed it up!" yelled the Little Red Car. "You lumbering great lorry, can't you wait until *I'm* not on the road?"

But a policeman on a motorbike was travelling with the lorry. Ooops! The Little Red Car went rather quiet.

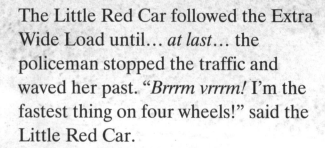

The Little Red Car followed the Extra Wide Load until… *at last*… the policeman stopped the traffic and waved her past. *"Brrrm vrrrm!* I'm the fastest thing on four wheels!" said the Little Red Car.

But suddenly…

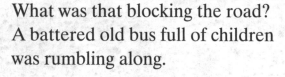

What was that blocking the road? A battered old bus full of children was rumbling along.

"Beep, beepity, BEEP! I don't believe it!" groaned the Little Red Car.

But the battered old bus just kept rumbling along.

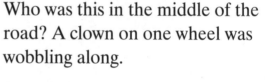

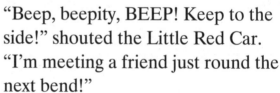

The Little Red Car brrrmed and beeped behind the battered old bus until… *at last*… it stopped outside a café and she could dash past. "*Brrrm vrrrm*! What a relief! I'm nearly there!" said the Little Red Car.

But suddenly…

Who was this in the middle of the road? A clown on one wheel was wobbling along.

"Beep, beepity, BEEP! Keep to the side!" shouted the Little Red Car. "I'm meeting a friend just round the next bend!"

Ooo… er… The clown on one wheel wobbled and wiggled and sat down with a BUMP in a bush.

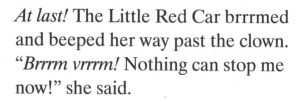

At last! The Little Red Car brrrmed and beeped her way past the clown. *"Brrrm vrrrm!* Nothing can stop me now!" she said.

But suddenly…

What was happening to the Little Red Car? With a *futt, futt, putt-putt-putt*, she came to a silent…

standing…

stop.

"Beep, beepity, BEEP! I've run out of petrol! I *thought* I had a funny feeling in my fuel tank," said the Little Red Car wearily.

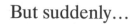

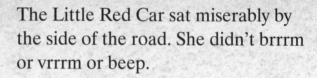

The Little Red Car sat miserably by the side of the road. She didn't brrrm or vrrrm or beep.

But suddenly…

Dring, DRING! The clown wobbled past on his one wheel.

Barp, BARP! The battered old bus rumbled past and all the children smiled and waved.

Toot, TOOT! The Extra Wide Load *and* the policeman moved slowly past.

Honk, HONK! The blue truck loaded full of tooters and hooters and bangers and clangers trundled past.

Peep, PEEP! The baker's van crawled carefully past.

Boop, BOOP! Last of all the tall truck full of blown-up balloons chugged slowly past.

Slow as a snail? Huh!

"I've been very silly," thought the Little Red Car. "With all my beeping and brrrming and vrrrming, I'm not surprised nobody wants to help me."

But suddenly…

Who was this wobbling on one wheel down the road? The clown was bringing a can of petrol and he was smiling all over his face.

"Come on, Little Red Car," he said. "Gary-at-the-Garage says we can't start without *you*!"

In no time at all the Little Red Car was filled up with petrol and…*at last*… she was on her way again.

And suddenly…

There was the truck and the baker's van and the blue truck and the Extra Wide Load and the battered old bus. And there were balloons and a birthday cake and a band and a bouncy castle *and* the policeman and the children and Gary-at-the-Garage with a great big smile on his face!

"Happy birthday, Little Red Car!" he grinned. "We couldn't start your party without *you*!" And everybody sang…

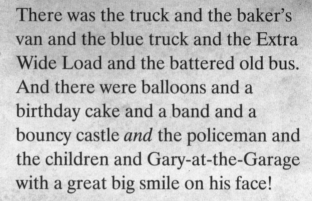

"Happy dring, barpety toot!
Happy honk, peepity boop!
Happy beep, beepity birthday,
Happy birthday to you!"

Gary's Garage

OIL AND PETROL

Happy Birthday - Little Red Car

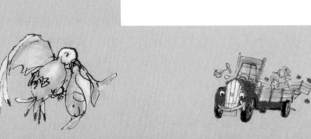

Noisy
Little
Truck

It was another beautiful day in the quiet little square.

Swish! Swoosh! The storekeeper swept the steps of her shop.

Snipper! Snip! The hairdresser busily whizzed with her scissors.

Splish! Splosh! High on a ladder, right at the top, a workman was painting the town hall clock.

There was not another sound to be heard.

But just then…

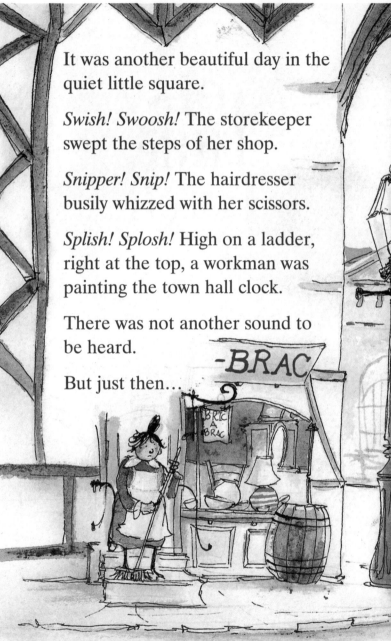

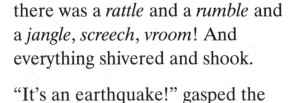

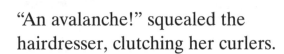

there was a *rattle* and a *rumble* and a *jangle*, *screech*, *vroom*! And everything shivered and shook.

"It's an earthquake!" gasped the storekeeper, diving for cover.

"An avalanche!" squealed the hairdresser, clutching her curlers.

"A disaster!" cried the workman, dropping his paint pot. "Look out below!"

But it wasn't an earthquake, or an avalanche, or a disaster. It was…

Look out below!

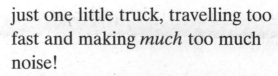

just one little truck, travelling too
fast and making *much* too much
noise!

The Little Truck braked with a
squeal and a *BEEP*!

"Important deliveries here for the
store! I'll be driving in daily to bring
you some more!"

"*Every* day?" asked the hairdresser,
faintly.

"We do *need* deliveries every day,"
sighed the storekeeper.

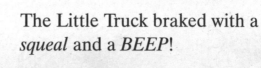

"What we *need*," said the painter, "is some *warning*. Why not come at lunchtime, Little Truck, when I'm *not* up my ladder? And a little less speedy, if you please."

"No problem!" called the cheerful Little Truck.

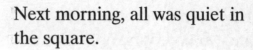

Next morning, all was quiet in
the square.

The painter finished the town hall
clock and set it going again. *Tick! Tock!*

The storekeeper chopped and
wrapped and weighed.

The hairdresser cut and curled
and sprayed.

At lunchtime, old Mr McCrumb came
out to feed the birds. And everyone
else sat down in the sun.

But just as the hairdresser poured
out her soup…

the painter picked up
his sandwich…

and the storekeeper
settled down for
a snooze…

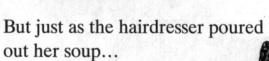

there was a *rattle* and a *rumble* and
a *jangle*, *screech*, *BEEP*! The noisy
Little Truck *did* try to drive with
more care, but *still* everything
shivered and shook.

The hairdresser's soup was spilled
with a *gloop*!

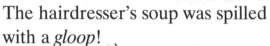

The painter's sandwich
dropped with
a *plop*!

Oh no!

And the storekeeper fell off her chair.

Not again!

The Little Truck parked.
"Was that better?" he asked.

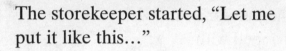
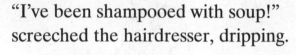

The storekeeper started, "Let me put it like this…"

"I've been shampooed with soup!" screeched the hairdresser, dripping.

"I've pilchards in my paint!" moaned the workman, fishing.

The Little Truck thought, "I've a brilliant idea! I'll come at a time when *no one* is here."

Next day, the square was quiet
and still.

No sandwiches jumped and no soup
was spilled.

But, when everyone was tucked up
in bed, at the very quietest time of
the night…

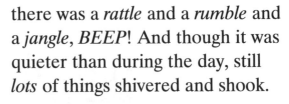

there was a *rattle* and a *rumble* and a *jangle*, *BEEP*! And though it was quieter than during the day, still *lots* of things shivered and shook.

Old Mr McCrumb tumbled *bump,* out of bed!

The painter's whole family woke up and said, "What was *that*?"

And the storekeeper opened her door with a *crash*!

"If that's you-know-who, it's not funny," she called. "I'm going to sort this out *once and for all*!"

So down in the square, in some *very* strange clothes, everyone gathered to grumble and groan.

"I'm sorry to say, all my pigeons have gone!" said old Mr McCrumb.

"*Something* must be done!" the hairdresser agreed.

"I *am* driving more slowly," said the noisy Little Truck, sadly. "I can't help *some* rumbling. I'm a *truck*, after all!"

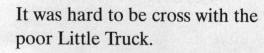

It was hard to be cross with the poor Little Truck.

"It *can't* really be easy, with a big, heavy load," agreed Mr McCrumb.

Then the painter's small daughter had her own bright idea. She stood on her tiptoes to reach her dad's ear.

She whispered. He listened. The whisper went round. And so did a smile as big as the town!

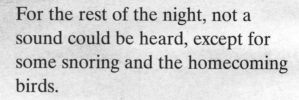

For the rest of the night, not a sound could be heard, except for some snoring and the homecoming birds.

Then, just as the sun slipped into
the sky…

there was a *rattle* and a *rumble* and
a *beep*, *beepity*, *BEEP*! At once the
whole town was awake.
"Well *done*, Little Truck," they all
came out to say.

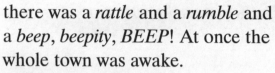

"Now we'll never be late to start each new day!"

Forgetful
Little
Fireman

Little Fireman Hugh of Fire Crew Number Two was having his breakfast. He was just pouring milk on his cornflakes when the fire station bell rang. *Ring a ding ding! Ring a ding ding!*

The fire chief stuck his head round the door.

"Hurry! Hurry!" he called. "We're needed at Polly's pet shop. The animals have got out and Polly can't find them."

There was no time to lose. Fire Crew Number Two sprang into action.

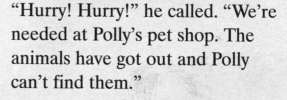
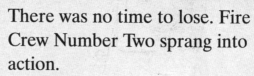
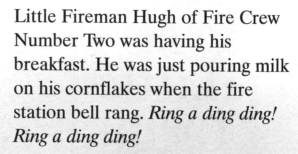

Little Fireman Hugh was first to slide down the pole. He jumped onto the red engine. But he was in such a hurry he'd forgotten something.

"Wait!" said the chief. "You can't go out in your socks!"

"Oh gadzooks!" cried Hugh. "I've forgotten my boots."

He rushed back upstairs. He pulled on his boots and slid down the pole.

"Hurry! Hurry!" called the chief. "We've got to rescue Polly's pets."

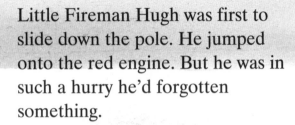
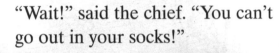

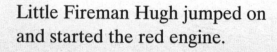

Little Fireman Hugh jumped on and started the red engine.

"Wait!" said the chief. "You can't go without your helmet!"

"Look at that!" cried Hugh. "I've forgotten my hat!"

Fireman Hugh flew back upstairs. He snatched his helmet and slid down the pole.

"Hurry! Hurry!" called the chief. "We've got to rescue Polly's pets."

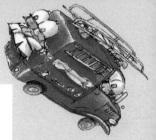

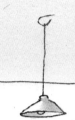

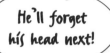

He'll forget his head next!

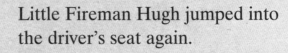

Little Fireman Hugh jumped into the driver's seat again.

This time he made sure that he'd got everything. "Got my helmet, got my boots, got my jacket. Let's go!"

He started the engine and drove off.

"Wait! Wait!" called the chief. "You've left ME behind!"

"Oh, good grief!" cried Hugh. "I've forgotten the chief!"

He looked back and saw the chief puffing down the road after them.

Come back!

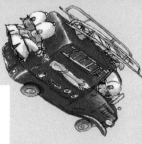

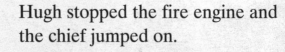

Hugh stopped the fire engine and the chief jumped on.

"*Now* let's go!" cried the chief. "We've got to rescue Polly's pets."

Little Fireman Hugh drove the engine fast through the streets.

"*WEE! WOO! Let me through!*" went the siren.

Cars stopped to let the fire engine go by. Fire Crew Number Two held on tight as they swung round corners and raced through the traffic.

At last they arrived at Polly's pet shop. Polly was waiting at the door.

"Thank goodness you're here," she said. "There was a storm last night and all the animals escaped from the pet shop. I've looked everywhere but I can't find them. What will I do if they don't come back?"

"Don't worry, Polly," said the chief. "They can't have gone far. Fire Crew Number Two will find them."

Fire Crew Number Two split up to search for Polly's pets.

Little Fireman Hugh looked in Polly's garden. He looked in the flower beds, he looked under bushes, he looked in the shed – but he didn't find any pets.

Then a voice squawked, "Who's a clever boy then?"

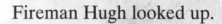

Fireman Hugh looked up.

"Bring the ladder," he called.
"There's a parrot in the pear tree."

Fireman Hugh climbed the ladder
and the parrot hopped onto his
shoulder.

Soon it was safely back in its cage.

Then Hugh had a look in Polly's house.

He looked in the cupboards, he looked up the chimney, he looked under the table – but he couldn't find any pets.

Then he heard a hissing sound coming from the kitchen…

It's one of Polly's pets!

I bet I know who it is!

"Help!" said Fireman Hugh.
"There's a snake in the sink!"

Carefully Fireman Hugh carried
the snake back to Polly. Soon it
was safely back in its box.

Next he went upstairs to look in the bedroom.

He looked behind the curtains, he looked in the wardrobe, he looked under the bed – but he didn't find any pets.

Then he heard snoring coming from under the bedcovers...

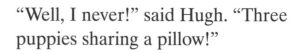

"Well, I never!" said Hugh. "Three puppies sharing a pillow!"

Soon the puppies were back in the shop along with all the other pets.

"There you are," smiled the chief. "I said they hadn't gone far."

"Thanks so much for finding my pets," said Polly. "The only one still missing is Tilda the tortoise. I do hope she isn't lost."

Well done, Fire Crew Number Two!

Where's that naughty tortoise?

"That reminds me," said Hugh, "I do beg your pardon. I think I left my helmet out in your garden."

Fire Crew Number Two all laughed. Trust Fireman Hugh to have forgotten something!

But when they all went out in the garden they saw something very strange. Hugh's helmet was crawling off down the path by itself...

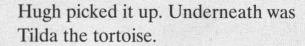

Hugh picked it up. Underneath was
Tilda the tortoise.

"Oh, how clever, you've found
Tilda!" said Polly and gave Hugh a
big kiss. Fireman Hugh blushed as
red as his engine.

Sometimes he didn't mind being a
little fireman who was a little
forgetful.